Contents

Misty

Misty

by Gillian Philip

'Now who—?' Thea did a double take and braked.

The man on the bypass wasn't your average hitchhiker. He was sharply dressed, in a well-cut suit and a blue-green silk tie.

Oh. Thea blinked. Of course: how had she forgotten that pile-up back there? Now she remembered the glimpse of crushed metal beyond the ambulances. How had this guy climbed out of that wreckage and staggered away? Maybe he'd been thrown clear. A head injury? He probably didn't know where he was. A bit lax of the paramedics.

Shaking her head, Thea glanced at her watch: only half eight. She pulled over and shoved open the passenger door.

'Can I take you to the hospital?'

Bending down, the man peered in at Thea. There was something familiar about him, but Thea couldn't place it. She couldn't place much this morning, with this headache. God, she felt awful. Vague and hungover. Should have called in sick.

He rubbed his forehead, smearing blood, then frowned as he looked at his fingers.

'That's good of you. You sure it's no trouble, er—?

'Thea. Thea Madeley. Here, get in. You look terrible.'

'I'm sure I do.'

The man sank gratefully into the passenger seat and tugged the door shut. When he turned to Thea, though, he wore an unexpected grin.

'D'you know, I just knew it was you. Soon as I saw your face through the car window, I thought: that's young Thea. One of my favourite pupils! Can't believe you're old enough to drive.'

'Passed my test a month ago.' Thea frowned. 'Sorry, but I—'

'Don't remember me? Well, you'd just started Year Eight when I left teaching. Must be – four years ago? Five?'

Thea blushed. God, what was wrong with her head this morning?

'Mr Munro! Media Studies! I'm sorry, I—'

'*Harry*, seeing as you've left school.

Haven't you?"

'Only this year. I've got a job on the *Eastwick Chronicle*. Just in the office, getting experience. I'm driving there now.'

'Oh. I hope this isn't an inconvenience.'

'No. It's only half eight.' Thea pulled out her phone and checked it. No messages. 'I can text if I'm going to be late. This is an emergency.'

'Watch the road, Thea,' said Harry, giving her a wry look.

'Oh, yeah. That was quite a smash back there. How'd it happen?'

'Don't know...' Harry frowned.

'Maybe I should call ahead to the hospital. We'll be there in ten minutes, but—' She peered at her phone again. 'No signal. Typical.' She prodded a button.

'Thea!' Harry tensed. 'Not while you're driving.'

'Relax.' She was completely in control, of course; Harry Munro was just on edge, and no wonder. 'I'm fine.'

'Good, good.' Harry still seemed nervous. 'Careful, Thea. There's mist in the valley ahead.'

'Oh, yes! That's where you'd expect a crash, not on the bypass. I mean, how do people manage to – sorry.' She blushed again. 'Sorry. Accidents happen, I guess.'

'I suppose.' Harry shrugged, then smiled. 'So how's the job, Thea?'

'Good! I mean, okay. It's a start.' She reddened.

It seemed less impressive, now that she'd remembered why Harry Munro left teaching. He'd gone to work for that young politician, the one who'd got everyone so excited a few years back. Passionate, sincere, charismatic: Britain's own JFK.

Matt Cornwell had come from their town – in other words, from out of nowhere. Thea remembered her dad going on about Cornwell, the way his voice filled with respect and his eyes shone. She remembered her mum actually crying about him.

She remembered it better than she remembered her own name, this morning. Fizzy water and orange juice tonight. Definitely.

'I saw you on TV once. A few years back. With that Matt Cornwell.'

'Just the once?' Harry teased.

'Well, I was young. Wasn't into politics.'

Harry gave a long, sad sigh.

'You're still young, Thea.'

Harry Munro had gone with Cornwell as his press officer, fixer, minder. He'd given him a stratospheric profile; run a dynamic campaign on the internet; terrified

journalists and charmed them all at once.
Together, Matt Cornwell and Harry
Munro had been heading for Number 10...

'Rotten that he died,' said Thea.

Her companion sighed again, as if the
memory was still painful. Harry had given
up everything for Matt Cornwell, hitching
his wagon to a shining shooting star. And
then the star had fallen. Extinguished
for good.

'When I think I could have been
running the country by now.'

'Behind the scenes, of course,' said Thea.

'Best way to do it,' laughed Harry.

Poor guy. The end of Matt Cornwell
must have been the end of Harry's
glittering future, too, because Thea was
sure she hadn't heard of him since. Harry
had the pallor of a man with a permanent
boring desk job. Mind you, if she could

get her head together she could interview him. Hey, a scoop!

'A plane crash, of all things,' mused Harry. 'It's almost a cliché.' He shook his head in melancholy wonder.

Not long now and they'd be at the hospital. Surely the *Chronicle* wouldn't mind her being late if she was finding a story? Thea glanced at her watch. Half past eight. But maybe she should check with the editor. Let him know. She checked her phone again. Still no signal.

'I wish you wouldn't do that,' said Harry.

'Don't worry,' said Thea, irritated. She added pointedly, 'Did a phone cause that crash?'

'I—' Harry frowned. 'You know, I think it might have done.'

'Well, it's not going to happen now.'

'No. Fair enough. Silly of me.'

Harry laughed, a genuine laugh that made Thea feel quite relieved.

'Ah, well. I'm not surprised you didn't remember me at first, Thea. Nobody ever does, not after Matt. Careful, now! We're getting pretty close to that mist. Oh, I'm doing it *again*!'

Thea shot him an understanding look. Of course he was a bundle of nerves. To humour him, Thea eased off the accelerator; but despite the mist lying in the valley, the road conditions were good up here and the air was clear. There weren't even many other cars on the road.

None, in fact. That was unusual, but she'd been the last to get through before the police blocked the road and set up a diversion. Well, she must have been. She assumed she was...

Thea punched the radio controls in

search of a traffic report, but a hissing white noise was all she could get. Wincing, she switched it off.

In the silence, she heard Harry humming cheerfully. For a guy in shock he seemed remarkably cool. Pale, but cool.

'I am glad I met up with you.' Harry gave her a smile. 'I was supposed to, you see. After the car crash and all. One of my old pupils!'

'Fate, you reckon?' said Thea lightly.

'You could say that,' agreed Harry. 'Fate.'

Thea eyed him nervously.

'You've got to meet it some time,' added Harry. 'However young.'

Thea swallowed hard. 'What a mess it was back there.' She didn't know why her voice was trembling, or why her spine was so cold. 'You're lucky you got out of it at all.'

'I didn't, Thea.'

Into the silence leaked a low white noise. *I thought I switched that off*, thought Thea. She punched the radio switch again, then again, harder. Harder. Frantically.

'Careful, Thea! Watch the road! *Honestly!*'

'What d'you – the crash.' Panic filled her. 'What d'you mean, *you didn't get out of it?*'

'Oh!' Harry chuckled. 'I didn't mean – oh, Lord, I'm sorry I scared you. I mean, I wasn't *involved* in the crash. You assumed that, of course. Sorry. No, no. That crash was nothing to do with me.'

Thea gave a high laugh, dizzy with relief. She felt silly and childish for even thinking it.

'Sorry. Being stupid. Imagination running away with me.'

'Oh, Thea. That's perfectly understandable. The circumstances are a little odd, aren't they? But no, no. I didn't get out of the crash.'

Thea's reply stuck in her throat. She wanted to ask where Harry had come from, then. Why he'd been there on the roadside. Why, when Thea looked desperately at her watch, it was still half past eight. But her voice had dried to ash.

'I didn't get out of that pile-up.' Harry's smile was apologetic now. 'And, um – neither did you.'

Thea stared at the cut on Harry's forehead. And then at the deep gash on his neck. Self-consciously Harry tightened his blue-green silk tie to cover it again, to steady his wobbling head.

'With me it was the plane, wasn't it? I was a bit of a postscript, mind you.' Harry rolled his eyes fondly. 'I was on the same plane as Matt Cornwell. Remember?'

The mist was almost on them. The road disappeared into it just ahead, and there were still no other cars. But she remembered now. His plane. Her car. She remembered everything.

'I didn't see a diversion!'

'There's no diversion, Thea. No detours. Look.' Harry tapped his hand affectionately on Thea's white one, on the fingers locked in terror round the steering wheel. He nodded ahead.

'We're going now, Thea. Do watch the road in this mist.'

Tunnel

Tunnel

by Dennis Hamley

It was already dark as the people left their houses and began the climb to the castle. They walked quietly but Tom felt tension in the air. The ominous wail of air raid warnings began before they reached the secret tunnels underneath Dover Castle. Their pace quickened so they would not hear the drone of the bombers.

It was 1940 and enemy bombers came

over every night. One tunnel, deeper than the rest, was reserved as an air raid shelter. It was called the Esplanade, which Tom thought was a pretty silly name. But it didn't matter: Dover Castle had watched over the Channel for seven hundred years. Invasions had been repelled and defences planned in those tunnels. Only a few months ago, the great rescue at Dunkirk was thought up in them, when most of the British army had been brought home from France by hundreds of little ships.

But not all. Tom's father was missing.

'Tom, keep close to me and Josie,' said Mum. Tom was twelve, his sister Josie seven. The tunnel was dark in spite of electric lights set in the wall. People jostled to find comfortable places.

'Yes, Mum,' Tom answered, but was soon

exploring the ends of the tunnel where the lights ended and the darkness was a curtain of deepest black.

'Who knows what's behind it?' said a voice beside him.

Tom jumped. Someone stood beside him, tall, draped in a hooded cloak. Its voice was a hoarse whisper. He could not tell whether it was a man or woman. He looked for a face, but only saw an even darker shadow under the hood.

'If only we could twitch the curtain aside.' The whisper again. 'The tunnel might stretch on for miles, empty. But it might be full of people that you do not know, longing for the light yet knowing that their duty must be done in the dark. So it has been for centuries.'

'I don't know what you're talking about,' Tom gasped.

'Twitch the curtain aside and see,' said the voice.

Even though they were in the lowest tunnel of all, Tom could hear the roar of planes, the whistle of falling bombs and explosions. He thought suddenly of his father. Was he dead? No, he'd never believe it. But a voice said, 'You must face it. He may be.'

Was it the strange figure again? He heard another whisper. 'Twitch the curtain.' And then the figure was gone.

Tom bit down a surge of fear and stepped forward. The weak lights of the tunnel were gone and blackness enveloped him.

He stood frozen with fright. He still heard the bombs and planes. *But how can I?* he wondered. *We're deep under the ground. You can't hear noises on top.* Before he worked out an answer, he heard the hoarse whisper again:

'Keep walking forward.'

There was nothing barring his way. His eyes got used to the darkness. Sensing that the way was clear, he walked forward almost confidently.

The floor became rougher and the walls lower. There was no smooth cement lining now: the tunnel looked hacked out by bare hands and shovels. A noise reached his ears, a terrible noise, faint at first but growing louder. Shouts, shrieks, cries of pain, bellows of fierce anger, the clang of metal on metal.

The noise grew until it was deafening. A weak, flickering light showed the way: he turned a corner – and there it was.

A fight. No, more than that: a terrible battle in this stifling, dark place. Flames of torches cast shifting patches of light and leaping, restless shadows. Men in chainmail and helmets struggled together. They hacked at each other with short swords and axes, screamed with rage like wild animals. The walls and floor were red with blood. The dead and wounded were trampled underfoot. Even as Tom watched, a man, screaming in helpless fury, was chopped down in front of him and a fount of blood gushed from his leg.

He felt he was seeing a horror film. The battle was behind a screen which he could never cross. *Well*, he thought, *they can't get me so it can stay like that. But who are they? Why am I seeing them?*

Once or twice he saw flags raised and shouts of, 'To me! To me!' At once, one side seemed to close together and a shout went up, 'De Burgh! De Burgh.' It

was answered by another: 'Prince Louis!'
And then the fight started again, fiercer
than ever.

Gradually Tom grew used to the horrors
and watched with interest, not fear – until
a group of struggling men seemed to sway
nearer to him, nearer, nearer – and then
he realised that the screen was down and
there was nothing between him and the
battle. He was part of it.

He felt the heat and sweat from their
bodies, winced as blows and jabs rained in.
One of the soldiers lunged at another with
a sword. He caught him on the shoulder
and the sword cut through the chainmail.
Blood welled from the wound and the man
crashed to the ground. He lay alone, because
already the struggle had moved away.

Horrified, Tom looked down at the man
writhing at his feet. He had to do something,

call for somebody, get help. But who?

Desperately, he bent down to the man.

'There's no one here to help except me,' he whispered. 'But I don't think I'll be much use.'

The man groaned and clutched his shoulder. Tom suddenly felt strength surge through him. He wrenched and pulled until the mailshirt was out of the way. Underneath, the man wore a rough tunic soaked in blood. Tom tore at it until he could see the wound.

What would Mum do?

'It's not so bad,' he told the man. 'I can stop it.'

He took out his handkerchief to staunch the blood until it was a trickle.

'Mum would put antiseptic on it,' he said. 'But I haven't got any.' He thought for a moment and then said, 'But I can bandage it up.'

He took his shirt off and tore a strip off the tail. He bound it tightly round the man's shoulder and said, 'That'll protect it a bit as long as it doesn't start bleeding again.'

The man stood up unsteadily. He took his helmet off. And then Tom gasped with shock. For the man's face was his father's.

'*Dad!*' he finally managed to stutter.

The man showed no recognition.

'I shall be well now,' he said.

His accent was strange, though Tom could just about make out the words. But, accent or no accent, *the voice was his father's.*

'Dad!' he cried again.

'I must go back to my comrades,' said the man. 'There's fighting still to be done to destroy the invader.'

He turned and walked away into the blackness. But before he disappeared he turned again and repeated, 'I shall be well now.' He looked at Tom straight in the eye and said, 'Do not fear. I shall return. Goodbye and thank you, Tom.'

Tom felt faint again. So the man *did* recognise him. Even as he wondered, the blackness seemed to die away, he was back in the Esplanade and the dark figure was next to him.

'Go back to your people,' it whispered. 'Your work is done.'

And then Tom was alone.

He found Mum and Josie.

'Where have you been?' Mum demanded angrily. 'What's on your hands? What have you done to your shirt?'

'I saw Dad,' he answered faintly.

'Don't be so stupid and don't make fun of something so serious. I thought better of you than that.'

'Mum, who's Prince Louis? Do you know anyone called de Burgh?'

'I don't know to the first question and no I don't to the second. You'll have to ask Mr Robins. He's in here somewhere. And don't change the subject. I haven't finished with you yet.'

But Tom had gone, searching through the crowds for Mr Robins, his form teacher.

He found him near the entrance to the Esplanade.

'Excuse me, sir,' he said. 'Who's Prince Louis?'

'What a strange thing to ask now,' Mr Robins answered.

'Why is it strange?'

'Because here we are fighting for our

lives and here's you asking about the last time Britain was invaded from across the Channel. And it's not 1066 in case you're wondering.'

'When was it then?' said Tom.

'It was 1216,' replied Mr Robins. 'That's over seven hundred years ago. Prince Louis of France brought an army across when the barons invited him to become king because they hated King John. Hubert de Burgh was warden of Dover castle. He beat the French back. Just think of it. The French had built tunnels under the castle to get inside and the battle was in the dark. Dreadful. I daren't think what it must have been like.'

I can, Tom thought.

'Thank you, sir,' he said and melted back into the crowd. As he walked, questions poured into his mind.

What have I seen? Why did I see it? Was that really Dad? How could he be fighting in a battle seven hundred years ago when he's in the army now? Why could I hear an air raid when I'm a hundred feet below ground? It's as if the new battle and the old battle are the same. Who was that dark figure who took me there and then said my work was over? What work?

He had no answers but as he returned to Mum and Josie, a thought was growing, stronger and stronger, until it burst out of his mind in a great shout.

'Mum, Dad's all right. He'll be coming home.'

Mum sighed. 'Please don't mock me. I've had enough of it and of you as well.'

'But he will. I know it.'

'How do you know, Tom?'

The all-clear sounded. Everybody trooped outside. There had been no air raid after all. The bombers had flown over looking for other targets The morning was as bright and fresh as if there wasn't a war on and never had been.

Tom smiled. 'I just do,' he said.

Three weeks later a letter arrived. It was from the War Office, with the news they had hardly dared to hope for. Dad had been taken prisoner. What ever else might happen to him, he was alive.

Mum cried with joy. So did Tom. But when they had dried their eyes, he said, 'I told you, Mum.'

Five years later, the war was over. Thousands of soldiers came home. And Dad was one of them. Two days after he arrived, he suddenly said, 'I was wounded at Dunkirk. A bullet in my shoulder. After

I was taken prisoner, I had a very strange dream. The German doctors were very good to me. They took the bullet out. I must have been drowsy after the anaesthetic, because I dreamt that it was you who bandaged me up.'

Tom smiled to himself. *It was*, he thought, though he never said it out loud.

The
Hanging
Tree

The Hanging Tree

by Anne Rooney

Shadows lay like crooked fingers over the path. They seemed to claw at the stones. Alfie wondered if they were clawing their way out or in. He looked up into the tree that cast the shadows. It troubled him more in winter than in summer. Those twig fingers, poking at the sky, their ghosts splayed on the path below. Alfie turned up his collar and pulled his scarf tight around his neck, covering the lower part of his face. He felt his breath damp and warm on the inside of the scarf.

'Why don't you like the tree?' Kayleigh asked, linking her arm through his.

'Do you think I don't like it?' he said.

Kayleigh laughed.

'It's obvious. You speed up to walk past it. And you sort of huddle up in your coat.'

It was true. Alfie hated the tree. He was sure on winter nights he had heard sounds coming from it. Rustling, even when there were no leaves. Or a low hissing that really couldn't be the wind.

'My grandfather told me about it,' he said.

'Tell me. I don't know any of the local tales,' Kayleigh said. 'I love that your family has always lived here. You know everything. Tell it to me as he told it to you.'

'It was more than two hundred years

ago. Jack Tippett hid in a copse of trees on the hilltop. He'd done it many times before. It was cold. His horse snorted clouds of steamy breath that mixed with the fog. At last, a stagecoach rumbled up the hill. Jack pulled his scarf up over his face so that just his eyes showed. He spurred his horse and galloped out in front of the coach. The coach horses reared up and whinnied in fright. Jack Tippett fired one of his three muskets in the air.

"Stand and deliver!" he shouted.'

'He was a highwayman?' asked Kayleigh.

'Yes. The people stumbled from the stagecoach, trembling. They emptied their pockets and purses. But it went wrong. There was a boy in the stagecoach, called Benjamin Lucas. He clung to his mother's skirts and stared wide-eyed at the highwayman. He looked into Jack's green eyes above the scarf. He saw the curved scar that ran through his eyebrow.

"Hello, Jack!" he called. And Jack fired his second musket into the boy's chest.'

Kayleigh shuddered.

'How horrible – he killed a little child?'

Alfie went on. 'Horrified at what he'd done, Jack turned his horse and galloped into the night. But next day, fourteen angry men were waiting for him. They beat him and bound him and dragged him to the tree – this tree. They tied a rope around his neck. Benjamin's uncle threw the end of the rope over a branch and hauled on it, dragging Jack Tippet up into the air. He struggled and kicked his legs. He went blue in the face; his tongue hung out. The men hit him with sticks and threw stones at him. Eventually he stopped struggling.

But Jack Tippett didn't die in the tree. It began to rain. Hard rain like iron rods pelted the men and drove them back to seek cover. The hanging tree was blasted by lightning. It split down one side, dropping Jack Tippett to the ground. He ran through the grey spears of rain, the noose around his neck and the rope trailing in the mud.'

'What happened to him?'

'No one knows. He ran and ran. People say he runs still. He can never find rest. Not unless he finds someone to take his place in the hanging tree. Someone must pay for the hurt done to Benjamin Lucas.'

Kayleigh shivered. 'But it's just a story,' she said.

'It's a true story.'

'What, even about him still wandering the Earth? Do you believe that?'

'No,' said Alfie. But he wasn't sure.

They were right by the tree. Kayleigh pointed ahead, just to the left of the path.

'Look! Alfie, look at that bird! What's it doing?'

Alfie peered into the fog. 'It's just a magpie.'

'One for sorrow,' said Kayleigh. 'What's it doing? Look, it's got something in its beak.'

Alfie looked again. Something gold glittered in the bird's beak. There was a red stone, too, sparkling.

'It's got a gold and ruby ring!' he said.

At his voice, the magpie flapped its wings and rose into the fog. But it didn't go far. It landed on a branch just above them. It took three steps sideways along the branch, then dipped its head. When it flew down again, its beak was empty.

'It must have put it in its nest,' said Kayleigh. 'Climb up and get it. Please.'

Alfie swallowed. He didn't want to refuse. He didn't want her to think he was scared.

'It's nearly dark,' he said. 'I won't be able to see properly. Look at the fog.'

'You'll be able to see gold,' she said. 'It will sparkle. Go on. Please. I'd love a gold ring.'

Alfie held out his arms.

'Look,' he said, 'I'm in my school clothes. They're not good for tree climbing.'

Kayleigh laughed.

'They'll be fine. Are you scared?'

'No!' he said. 'But… No, of course not. I just don't think I'll be able to climb in these.'

Kayleigh touched his cheek. Her fingers were soft and cool.

'Please get it for me.'

Alfie dropped his school bag on the ground but he still didn't move. They stood looking at each other. Then Kayleigh threw down her own bag on top of his.

'Fine,' she said. 'I'll get it myself. I'm not scared of a stupid magpie. Or a tree.'

'I'm not scared,' Alfie protested. But it was too late. She was already pulling herself up, fingers twined around the thick stems of ivy that strangled the trunk. He stood watching, not sure what to do.

'Careful,' he called.

She looked over her shoulder at him. It was a disdainful look that made him embarrassed. She carried on climbing.

A flurry of ivy leaves fell to the ground in front of Alfie. At the same time, Kayleigh cried out.

'What is it?' he asked, peering upwards.

Kayleigh whimpered, stifling a sob. Her left foot was at an awkward angle, her right foot scrabbling for a foothold a little above his head, her fingers gripping the ivy.

'Are you OK?' he asked.

'No. I've hurt my ankle. My foot's stuck and I twisted it. *Owwww*,' she whimpered again. Alfie thought she would cry.

'Do you want me to help you?' he asked.

'Yes, please. Help me down and then get the ring.'

'What? You still want it?' He was angry now. It was a stupid thing to do, climb the hanging tree in the dark and the fog just for a ring. Couldn't she see now that it was stupid?

'I was just unlucky. You're good at climbing – you'll be fine.'

'Hang on. I'll get you down at least.' He had no intention of getting the ring, though.

He dug his fingers into cracks in the bark between the ivy and pulled himself up. The bark was wet and slippery with fog. But the tree wasn't hard to climb. Six feet above the ground it forked and after that branches came thick and fast.

Kayleigh was just past the fork. He soon reached her. He guided her right foot on to a solid branch, then gently lifted her left foot out of her shoe. She cried out as he twisted it, but then it was free and he showed her where to put it. He tossed the shoe to the ground and waited while she climbed down, guiding her to handholds as she passed him.

'Thank you,' she said, as her feet touched the ground. 'Can you see the nest?'

'Are you mad? Hasn't it been enough trouble already?'

'Go on Alfie, please! You aren't scared are you? You're almost there now.'

What could he do? If he refused, she'd tell everyone he was scared. She wouldn't like him any more. It would only take a minute.

The place the bird had landed was to his left. It was in a bare part of the tree that forked and jutted out over the space below.

45

Alfie pulled himself up to the branch and inched along it. He could see an untidy, dark shape through the gloom. It must be the nest. Twigs from above caught in his hair and snagged his clothes. They scratched his face and snatched at his hood. He shuffled along the branch, carefully, slowly.

'Hsssss.'

Alfie's neck prickled. He looked down at Kayleigh. She was beneath, looking up at him. Silent. What sound do magpies make?

'Hsssss.' There it was again – like a hiss or a whisper. Was he imagining it? He tried to look around, to see if there was someone else there.

But the magpie was back. It flew at his face making him jump. He lurched backwards, and had to grab at the branch so that he didn't fall. The bird flapped its wings at him and made a loud chattering sound, trying to drive him away.

Alfie tried to shuffle back along the branch, but he felt something cold and sharp poke at his neck. He twisted his head quickly but it only jabbed him harder. He couldn't turn his head back. Whatever had caught him was under his scarf. Rising panic made him wriggle. That made it worse. He raised a hand to his neck, but couldn't reach behind him. And the magpie flew at him again, straight at his face. He thrashed at it, but lost his balance. He snatched at the branch. His hand touched something hard and cold – something that moved away under his hand. He snatched his hand away again.

'Hsssss.'

Alfie teetered on the branch. The magpie flew at his face again, and he swiped wildly at it.

'Be careful!' shouted Kayleigh.

He twisted round at her voice, and the scarf tightened. He felt his leg sliding over the branch and into empty space. He grabbed at the branch, but his hand closed on nothing as he fell…

Then he jerked to a halt. All his muscles jolted. He couldn't breathe. His scarf pulled tight around his neck. He reached up with his hands but he couldn't loosen it – his body weight pulled it tight. He kicked and struggled, his feet flailing around in the air seeking a branch. But there were no branches, just open, empty air and the ground far below. He saw Kayleigh's mouth open to a scream.

The pain in Alfie's neck and chest was unbearable. He gasped desperately for breath but none came.

Suddenly, something gripped Alfie's wrist. Something icy and sharp, and brittle as twigs.

The surrounding darkness closed in on him and he stopped struggling.

'*Shhhhh.*'

It seemed that the fog itself whispered to him.

Another hand grabbed his shoulder. The fingers were so thin they felt like knife blades. They dug deep into Alfie's flesh. He felt like meat hung on a meat hook. Dead meat. That's what he was. But then he was rising through the air. Yes, surely he was rising? The meat hooks were lifting him up into the tree. The pressure on his neck became less.

One hand released him, the other digging further into his flesh as it took his weight.

Alfie tried to protest, but he had no breath. Then in front of his face, he saw half a grey-white face with spaces where the eyes should be and black hair hanging in tatters over and around it. The bottom half of the face was hidden. Was it behind a scarf? Or was it eaten away by the fog, or worse? Alfie couldn't tell. He felt something cold at his neck, something besides the wet scarf. Metal. A blade. He tried again to kick and flailed his legs. He struggled to get his free hand to his throat.

'Hsssss.'

That sound again, but right beside his ear this time.

The blade nicked his neck. It was icy cold, colder than ice. The coldest thing he had ever felt. The tightness at his neck eased a little, and then a little more. And then it was gone. Two halves of the scarf fell to the ground and then something else, something that made a dull sound as it hit the leaves. The meat hooks were back in his flesh, in both his wrists now. Alfie gulped in huge gasps of air, filling his empty lungs. His head was swimming, he felt faint. All he could see was the half face, its empty eye sockets windows on to the darkness behind.

'*Hsssss.*'

Alfie whimpered.

'Wh– what are you?' he managed to say.

'*Hssssss,*' it whispered. And then, very quietly, '*Jack.*'

The meat hook fingers lowered Alfie and then they were gone. He fell to the ground. The wet leaves were thick and cold beneath him. At once, the magpie rose into the air, and Kayleigh was beside him.

'Are you all right? What happened? I was so scared. I thought you'd be strangled!'

Alfie didn't answer. The tree loomed above him, a sprawling black shape against the fog. A patch of thicker fog seemed to hang in the tree. He thought he heard a sound again, '*Hsssss*.' But he couldn't be sure.

He saw, above him, the magpie with the ring in its beak once again. It stood on a branch and looked at him, cocking its head to one side.

Alfie put his hand out to push himself up. It met something thin, and colder than the leaves. His fingers closed on the blade and he picked it up. A folding knife.

'What happened?' Kayleigh said again.

'Jack,' Alfie said. 'He's paid his debt.' He held out his hand, the knife lying in his palm. The bone handle was worn and scratched, but he could just make out the initials carved into it: J.T.

The Waiting Room

The Waiting Room

by Alex Stewart

'Ghosts?' William's uncle looked up from the morning paper, where he'd been reading an account of the zeppelin raids on the capital with faint tuts of disapproval. A quizzical expression appeared between his thinning brown hair, and the clerical collar his nephew had never seen him without. 'Why do you ask?'

'I thought I saw something in the drawing room last night,' William said, pensively stirring the kedgeree on his plate. He'd been disturbed by the droning of airship engines passing over the sleepy Norfolk village, where Uncle Wilberforce had been rector since before he was born, and been unable to get back to sleep; his mother and sister Charlotte were still in London, and he feared for their safety every time he heard the sinister rumbling overhead. 'I went downstairs to get a book, but when I walked in, it all seemed different somehow.'

'In what way different?' Uncle Wilberforce asked, sounding intrigued. He folded the paper, and laid it on the breakfast table between them.

'I'm not sure,' William admitted, giving up on the kedgeree. The vision, or whatever it was, had lasted less than a second; then he'd blinked, and the room had returned to normal, leaving only a fleeting impression of whiteness and shadows in the moonlight. 'It was probably just a dream.'

'Probably,' Uncle Wilberforce agreed, with a faint air of relief. 'There are stories, of course, as with any old house, but I've never taken much notice of them. It would take a singularly bold spectre to haunt the home of a clergyman.'

'I suppose so.' William pushed the plate aside. Kedgeree was one of his favourites, and he was sure his uncle's cook had prepared it specially, but he didn't have much of an appetite this morning.

Uncle Wilberforce sighed sympathetically.

'I'm sure this is frightfully dull for you,' he said. 'Frittering your summer away with an old fossil like me.'

'Not at all,' William said. 'I've always enjoyed visiting here.' And that was true.

But on every previous occasion his parents

had been with him. This time, his father was somewhere in France, and he knew all too well what that meant: before the last term had ended, barely a week had gone by without the headmaster standing solemnly before the whole school at morning prayers, reading out the names of former pupils cut down by the German guns. Some of the fallen he'd even known, boys only a year or two older than himself, who had left their studies to enlist as soon as they could. His father's letters were always cheerful, but William wasn't fooled, receiving each one with a rush of relief, mingled with the dread that it might be the last.

'I'm delighted to hear it,' Uncle Wilberforce said, rising from the table. He smiled again, looking far younger than his years. 'My next sermon is almost completed, so I don't suppose the Almighty would take it amiss if we went fishing this morning instead of finishing it off.'

'Neither do I,' William agreed.

He followed his uncle out into the hall, then, moved by an impulse he couldn't explain, turned aside to walk into the drawing room. As he crossed the threshold he glanced round, and exhaled, only aware as he did so that he'd been holding his breath.

The room looked exactly like it always did, light and airy now that the curtains had been drawn, and the french windows opened to admit the clean country air. His uncle's books were neatly shelved, and the armchairs looked invitingly comfortable, ranged about the fireplace for warmth in the depths of winter. Anywhere less likely to be touched by the supernatural was hard to imagine.

Finally convinced that last night's transformation was no more than the memory of a dream, William was on the verge of leaving, when he caught sight of the mirror over the mantlepiece. The room it reflected seemed odd, although he couldn't quite tell why from this angle, and he took a pace or two towards it, trying to get a clearer view.

There was no doubt about it; instead of the familiar striped wallpaper, the walls in the reflection were white and smooth. Before he could make out any more detail a figure moved in the depths of the mirror, a girl he'd never seen before, but who somehow looked vaguely familiar, and he spun round to look behind him, straight at where she should have been standing.

The hairs on the back of his neck began to prickle: there was no one there, but a patch of dark air, swirling like smoke, grew from the carpet like a malformed bush. At the same time he became aware of a faint humming sound, like a swarm of bees in the distance.

'William. Are you all right?' Uncle Wilberforce stood in the doorway, his fishing tackle in his hands. 'I thought I heard you shout.'

'It's nothing,' William said. The mirror had gone back to reflecting the real room, the patch of shadow had gone, and there was no sign that anything had ever been amiss. If he tried to tell his uncle what he'd seen, he'd sound like a lunatic. 'Let's go fishing.'

As he led the way through the French windows into the garden, he realised that he could still hear the buzzing sound. If anything, it sounded even louder out here, and seemed to be growing in volume with every passing second.

'Merciful heavens,' Uncle Wilberforce said in astonishment, his rod and basket falling unheeded to the grass at his feet.

Looking up, William felt the breath catch

in his throat. Though he'd never seen one before, there could be no mistaking what it was. A vast, grey cigar shape, with whirling propellors sticking out from the cabin beneath it on the ends of long metal girders.

'A zeppelin,' he said. 'But why is it so low?'

'Because it's in trouble,' his uncle said, pointing. 'It must have been hit by the guns around London. Look.' A thin trail of smoke was visible from one of the engines, growing thicker and blacker with every passing second.

William shivered, as the vast shadow swept over them, the sinister grey shape almost directly above by now. As he watched, a red flower bloomed amid the smoke, and began to spread with astonishing rapidity as the flames leapt from the ailing engine to the gas-filled bag. The huge craft lurched, ablaze from end to end in a matter of moments, and began to fall.

Instinctively, William turned and ran, diving

back through the French windows, hoping to find some measure of safety inside the house. Impelled by panic, he'd taken several steps before he realised that the room was completely different from the one he'd just left.

Astonished, he stopped, and looked around, unable to believe the evidence of his own eyes. The walls were white, like the reflection he'd seen in the mirror, and the bookshelves had gone. So had the armchairs, and the occasional table; instead, a soft-looking couch, upholstered in the same floral print as the curtains which had sprouted by the French windows, stood in the centre of the polished wooden floor which had somehow replaced the carpet. The fireplace had gone, to leave the couch and a pair of matching chairs ranged around a large box with a glass front, the purpose of which he couldn't imagine.

'This part of the house was completely

rebuilt,' a voice said, and he turned to face the door, through which a middle-aged woman and the girl from the mirror were walking. They were both dressed like workmen, in blue trousers and long-sleeved shirts without collars; neither had buttons down the front, and William could see no sign of how they were fastened.

'I imagine so,' the girl said, brushing her hair out of her eyes as she spoke. 'I've seen photographs of the wreck.' She smiled. 'You're very kind to let me impose on you like this.'

'Excuse me,' William said, stepping forward to greet them, his head spinning. 'I don't understand what's happening here—'

'That's quite all right,' the woman said, and William realised she was still addressing the girl, ignoring him completely. 'If I had an incident as dramatic as that in my family history, I'd want to research it as well.'

'My great grandmother Charlotte was supposed to be here too,' the girl said, 'but she was delayed in London, campaigning with the suffragettes. Otherwise she'd have died, along with her uncle and her brother.'

'That's me!' William shouted, bewildered, but determined to attract their attention. 'And I'm fine! Look!'

'Lucky for you,' the woman said. 'Or you wouldn't be here either.'

'I suppose not.' The girl glanced briefly in William's direction, shivered, and returned her attention to her hostess. 'It must feel strange, knowing your house has a history like that.'

The woman laughed, and walked though William as though he was nothing more than a wisp of smoke.

'Well, I'm not superstitious,' she said. 'And who believes in ghosts these days anyway?'